THE GREAT WAR ENDED IN 1918. FARMERS ACROSS THE WESTERN FRONT CLEAR AWAY ROUGHLY 900 TONNES OF EXPLOSIVES EVERY YEAR.

THE COLD WAR ENDED IN 1991. WE DO NOT KNOW HOW MANY UNEXPLODED "BOMBS" ARE STILL OUT THERE.

OR WHO, IF ANYONE, IS CLEARING THEM AWAY.

ISSIONS

JED MCPHERSON
WRITER/LETTERER

MARCO PERUGINI
ARTIST

SHANNON BENNION
COLOURIST

CHRIS SHEHAN
VARIANT COVER

NEIL GIBSON
EDITOR

CHAPTER ONE

THE NUMBERS
STATION

GLOUCESTERSHIRE

*TRANSLATED FROM RUSSIAN.

CHAPTER ONE
[END]

CHAPTER TWO
DEAD AIR

CHAPTER TWO

[END]

CHAPTER THREE
PLAUSIBLE DENIABILITY

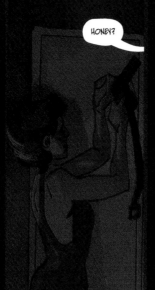

HEATHROW AIRPORT

*"CHARLIE... CHARLIE...

*"CHARLIE, C'MON. THEY'RE CALLING OUR FLIGHT."

WHAT?

WE GOTTA GO.

SHIT, I TOTALLY SPACED OUT.

JESUS, CHARLIE YOUR NOSE.

I'M ALRIGHT. JUST GET ME ON THAT FUCKING PLANE.

SHEREMETYEVO INTERNATIONAL AIRPORT.

CHAPTER THREE

[END]

CHAPTER FOUR
OVER

C'MON YOU ASSHOLE.
I'M RIGHT HERE. WHAT'RE YOU WAITING FOR?
JESUS, SASHA. WHAT THE HELL ARE YOU DOING?
I'M PLAYING A HUNCH.
LOOKS LIKE IT'S ALL CLEAR.
C'MON, LET'S GET OUT OF HERE.
I NEED A FUCKING DRINK.

*TRANSLATED FROM RUSSIAN.

"I'LL BE IN TOUCH."

OK, WHERE ARE WE ON BERLIN?

WE TRACED THE NERVE AGENT. IT'S DEFINITELY MILITARY GRADE.

VAUXHALL CROSS, LONDON

BUT WE CAN'T PROVE IT WAS THE RUSSIANS.

GOT IT IN ONE.

GODDAMNIT, I SWEAR IT USED TO BE EASIER THAN THIS.

ANYTHING ELSE?

THE NEW SECTION CHIEF STARTS TODAY.

TOO SOON IF YOU ASK ME.

IT'S BEEN SIX MONTHS. C CAN ONLY COVER OPS FOR SO LONG.

STILL, IT JUST DOESN'T SEEM LONG ENOUGH.

YEAH. SINCLAIR WAS ONE OF THE GOOD ONES. PLAYED THE GAME LIKE NO OTHER. TRUTH TOLD I FEEL *SORRY* FOR THE NEW GUY.

Charles Strafford
Section Chief

THANKS JACK.

Charles S
Section

YOU'LL DO FINE.

[END TRANSMISSION]

CONFIDENTIAL

A behind the scenes look at the making of Transmissions.

ANATOMY OF A COMIC PAGE

Unlike film or television or even prose there's no standard way to produce comics.* So, we thought it might be interesting to show you exactly how we made Transmissions.

It starts with the script. We break down each page into panels. Each panel into a description and dialogue and then redraft until we get something that we're happy with.

I then send this to Neil and he makes notes. We then go back and forth until we get something that we're both happy with.

Page two

Panel one

Move to a shot of Charlie as he chases The Operator down the flat's hallway. He has his gun at the ready.

About halfway down the corridor there's a family trying to unlock their flat door. They are looking up at the two men in surprise/ fear.

No copy

Panel two

Cut to a shot of The Operator as he pushes his way into the stairwell. The Operator is moving quickly almost mechanically.

Charlie's adrenaline is up. He's ready for a fight.

No copy

Panel three

Medium on Charlie as he pushes past the family, sending their shopping bags tumbling to the floor.

1. **Charlie:** Goddamnit. Move!

Panel four

Move to a shot of The Operator as he runs up the stairs. He's moving quickly, skilfully, like a freerunner.

No copy

Panel five

Hold the shot as Charlie looks up the stairwell in surprise as The Operator continues to sprint up the stairs.

1. **Charlie:** Jesus Christ.

Fig 1. It starts with the script. Jed writes descriptions for each panel and rough dialogue.

Then we send the script to Marco and he roughs out the pages and sends them back.

Once we see the pages I'll go through them and rough letter them using a program called Comiclife. Seeing the pages with the lettering at this point helps us identify any pacing issues, any miscommunication between artist and writer, and head off any story telling issues before Marco starts inking.

After I've finished rough lettering I'll schedule a call with Neil to go over the book with him and then we'll ask Marco to make any revisions required.

* When working on his own comics Neil writes his scripts in Excel like an absolute lunatic.

Fig 2. Then Marco sends over the roughs and Neil annotates them in comiclife looking for any parts that can be improved.

With pencils approved Marco moves onto inking. It's really at this stage the book really starts to look like a finished product.

Neil will then go over the book again, looking to make sure that any notes have been addressed. He may request one last round of changes but they should really only be minor tweaks at this point.

Fig 3. After making the requested changes Marco sends over the inks for approval. If everything checks out they're sent on to Shannon for colours.

Fig 4. Here's the final page after Shannon's colours. All that's left now is the lettering.

And here's the page with Shannon's colours. Shannon adds a lot of texture to the page, adding in the graffiti and really giving the book depth.

Colour is particularity important in this book. Not only does it help the tone but we also keyed the Numbers Station brainwashing to the colour red. Shannon was great at this. Often subtly using red to foreshadow a character falling under the influence of the numbers station.

Once we've got the colours for the entire book Neil and I will go through it one last time focusing on clarity and tone.

Then, when everything is approved I'll pick the book back up and start on the lettering. As I letter the book myself I tend to do a final pass over the dialogue at this point. Changing phrasing or even deleting sections to better suit the art.

Finally the book is proofed (mostly by the excellent Linda Canton) and then we're ready to print.

CODE MONKEY

Research is an important part of my creative process. So, when I decided to write a book about the numbers station I went heavy into cryptography. I got lost in a world of one time pads, substitution codes, and random number generators. And all of it was going into Sasha's introduction. She was going to look smart even if it was going to kill me.

But when I sent the script to Neil he took one look at that scene and aksed me to cut it. The book isn't really about codes or code breaking and having a big info

Fig 5. Far from being a random string of numbers the radio messages actually have a hidden message.

dump killed the pacing of the first issue and undercut Sasha's introduction.

Really it was just a way for me to show off how clever I was. Which is an instinct that I have to constantly fight against. (I actually have a post it note stuck to my monitor that says "just because you know things it doesn't make you interesting" to remind myself not to be a know-it-all dullard).

I rewrote the scene and left most of my research on the cutting room floor. But that left me with a lot of knowledge about codes and code breaking and nowhere to put it.

So, I did the only reasonable thing. I came up with a code of my own, keyed to something that is unique to comics, and hid it somewhere in the comic.

If anyone manages to break it shoot us an email at info@tpub.co.uk and Neil will make it worth your while.

Fig 6. I'm just going to leave this panel here. It has nothing to do with the code. I promise.

I've always had a DIY attitude towards making comics. I've lettered my own books, done book design, and I've even tried drawing a book (no you cannot see it and yes it was very, very bad).

I believe that all comic writers should try their hand at all aspects of the production of comics. I'm always trying to be a better collaborator and the more of the process I understand the better I can prepare my scripts.

That said, I want my books to look as professional as possible which often means that I have to hand off production to professionals (hence why you'll never see a book coloured by me).

So, while I played around with the logo design I always thought that the best case scenario was that I'd have a prototype logo. Something that I could show to a real designer and say "like that but better."

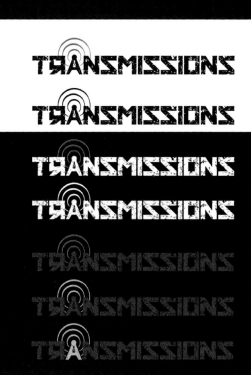

Fig 8. The final sheet. Demonstrating how the logo works with different colours/ backgrounds.

Fig 7. The WIP sheet I sent to Neil after he told me he didn't like the font I used for the original version.

But by the time I'd actually finished with it I was happy enough with it to send it on to Neil.

Now, Neil being Neil had some suggestions but with his feedback (and a few pointers from TPub's Sarah Meeks and my friend Zorika Gaeta) we came up with something that I feel expresses the book's themes well and looks pretty nifty to boot.

- Jed

COVER GALLERY

MARCO PERUGINI &
SHANNON BENNION

CHRIS SHEHAN

MARCO PERUGINI &
SHANNON BENNION

MARCO PERUGINI &
SHANNON BENNION

MARCO PERUGINI &
SHANNON BENNION

BACKERS:

Without the support of our amazing Kickstarter backers this book would not exist. On behalf of the entire creative team I would like to extend heartfelt thanks to all of you;

Nick Bryan - Ben Quinlan - Michael Nimmo - Gary Varga - - Linda J Canton - Michail Dim. Drakomathioulakis - Paul y cod asyn Jarman - Ken Nagasako - Asa Wheatley - Amrit Birdi - Léon Othenin-Girard - Chelsea Eggleton - Jonathan Azzopardi - Katie Fruin - Joe Whitfield - Bart-Jan Kuiper - Mark Anderson - Chris - Anthony Rivera - Kat Willott - Emerson Kasak - Aaron Gillians - Mika Koykka - Christian Meyer - John Ward - Denise Chung - Arianna & Laurence Shapiro - Bobby T - Jennifer Campney - Colin Wood - Barb - William Carranza - Dave Cook - Rothmeier - William Lohman - Alan Heighway - Jaap van Poelgeest - John Lamar - Pierre Mooser - Bobby Tilley - Troy Davis - Ali Burns - Glen McFerren, M.D. - Ryan Little - Gerald - Olivier - Izaac Walton - Conor H. Carton - Rusty Waldrup - Mike Gerth - Eli Morgan - Shawn Dean - Solly Danno - Rick Quinn - Frank Worley - Scott - Chris Miranda - Jason Crase - Steph Cannon - Roger Stone - Xavier Hugonet - Al Sims - Mark Featherston - Dave Kastner - Andrew McPherson - Karl Amspacher - Jack Holder - Chris Shehan - Joeri Overheul - Ralph Lachmann - Chris - Matyas Kadlicsko - Harrison Lee Kassen - Susan Grimes - Chris Newell - Sara Yearsley - Rachel H Sanders - Cody Sousa - Eugene Alejandro - Pete Davies - Christopher Wheeling - D. William Patton, Esq. - Jonathan Swanson - Eric Dugal - daniel enriquez - Annie Nate Schindler - Russell Turner - Eliza Keating - Juicebax - Matthew Shiell - Michael Easterwood - EDDY - Jamie Bright - Quicksilver_Rain - Kenny - Ben Collins - Jen Hogan - Vincent Guthrie - Crystal Weber - Kalai - Elizabeth Keith - Richard Linton - Jack Watkins - Gavin Call - Phillip Maira - Chelsea Rose - Nuno XEI - James Moore - Kellie Thompson - Fredrik Holmqvist - Sean Carson-Hull - Bob Smay - @JamesFerguson - Kristian Horn - Jay Lofstead - Charles Moulton - Shane Lowe - ro lamb - Evan Summers - Switch - STUART HENDERSON -Zack Quaintance - The Visual Time Keeper - Tony Cooper - Dan Mallier - Heroes By The Pint - Edwin Docherty - SwordFire - R.P. Sullivan - Dallas M Foard - Eric Hendrickson - Mark Judd

Other Titles from Twisted Comics

Twisted Dark
Volume 1

Twisted Dark
Volume 2

Twisted Dark
Volume 3

Twisted Dark
Volume 4

Twisted Dark
Volume 5

Twisted Dark
Volume 6

Twisted Dark
Volume 7

Twisted
Light

The Theory
Volume 1

Theatrics
Volume 1

Theatrics
Volume 2

The Traveller

Transmissions

Transdimensional

Turncoat

Disposable
Legends

Tabatha

The World of
Chub Chub!

Stan Lee's Lucky
Man

Tortured Life

NEIL GIBSON'S

COMICS

twistedcomics.com

JED MCPHERSON IS A COMIC WRITER. HE'S MOSTLY KNOWN FOR DEADBEAT: A NEO NOIR THRILLER ABOUT A DEADBEAT DAD TRYING TO RECONNECT WITH HIS DAUGHTER THROUGH ARMED ROBBERY.

BUT HE DOESN'T JUST WRITE CRIME COMICS HE'S ALSO WORKED ON THE SHOW – A DERANGED REALITY-TV SATIRE KIND OF LIKE THE TRUMAN SHOW AS ENVISAGED BY HUNTER S. THOMPSON.

YOU CAN FIND OUT MORE ON HIS SITE JEDMCPHERSON.COM. THERE ARE COMICS THERE. YOU'LL PROBABLY LIKE IT.

MARCO PERUGINI IS AN ILLUSTRATOR. HE'S WORKED FOR COMPANIES INCLUDING NOKIA, FOX, D&G, IBM, IVECO AND RAI.

HIS COMICS WORK INCLUDES MORGAN LOST FOR ITALIAN PUBLISHER SERGIO BONELLI. HE'S ALSO WORKED WITH INTERNATIONAL PUBLISHERS, INCLUDING EVOLUZIONE PUBLISHING AND HEAVY METAL.

ASIDE FROM COLOURING TRANSMISSIONS, SHANNON MOSTLY WORKS FREELANCE WHILST WORKING ON HER ORIGINAL CONCEPTS, ALL OF WHICH LEAN HEAVILY INTO SCI-FI/FANTASY AND THRILLER GENRES. SHE'S CURRENTLY WORKING ON AN ORIGINAL GRAPHIC NOVEL CALLED IF WE SHADOWS.

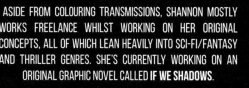

NEIL GIBSON IS A COMIC BOOK AUTHOR AS WELL AS THE EDITOR AT TPUB COMICS. HE HAS A STRONG PASSION FOR THE COMIC BOOK MEDIUM AND ITS POTENTIAL FOR COMMUNICATING AND LOVES COACHING NEW CREATORS IN THE INDUSTRY. HE HAS WRITTEN 10 GRAPHIC NOVELS INCLUDING THE BESTSELLER TWISTED DARK.

HE LIVES IN LONDON WITH HIS WIFE AND CHILDREN AND SEEMINGLY ENDLESS HOUSE GUESTS.

Did you enjoy the comic?

There are plenty more titles available
on our website or in comic shops, but if
you want some behind-the-scenes
material, please support Neil on **Patreon.**

Not only you do get access to
advance artwork, first look at
scripts and videos of the creative process,
but you also get invited to our writing
sessions where you can see how we
make the comics and be actively
involved in shaping future stories.

Head over to
patreon.com/NGTwistedComics
or scan the QR code